GW00858460

*Other North-South picture books*
*illustrated by* Nathalie Duroussy:

Little Moon
The Crystal Ball

Copyright © 1995 by Nord-Süd Verlag AG, Gossau Zürich, Switzerland
First published in Switzerland under the title *Schatzsuche und Finderglück*
English translation copyright © 1995 by Rosemary Lanning

All rights reserved.
No part of this book may be reproduced or utilized in any form
or by any means, electronic or mechanical, including photocopying,
recording or by any information storage and retrieval system
without permission in writing from the publisher.

First published in Great Britain, Canada,
Australia, New Zealand and Japan in 1995 by North-South Books,
an imprint of Nord-Süd Verlag AG, Gossau Zürich, Switzerland.

ISBN 1 55858 378 5

1 3 5 7 9 10 8 6 4 2

Printed in Belgium

# Treasure Hunt

Antonie Schneider

Nathalie Duroussy

Translated by Rosemary Lanning

North-South Books London

"All right, back there?" asked Mary, pulling
her brother along in a little cart. It was the first
day of their holiday, and Mother had sent them
out to buy milk.

Joe didn't answer. He had just seen something
amazing. Ahead of them, in amongst the
trees, stood a big blue ship, anchored to the
ground with thick ropes.

"A pirate ship," whispered Joe, with a shiver
of excitement.

A boy was standing in the ship's look-out post. He had a black bandana tied round his head and looked just like a pirate. "Ship ahoy!" he shouted. "Get ready to go aboard!"
"Can I play?" asked Joe, eagerly, scrambling up a ladder.

But when Joe looked around the ship, the boy with the bandana had disappeared. Everything was quiet.

"Joe! Look out!" cried Mary, suddenly, from below. Too late! A hard push sent Joe tumbling to the ground.

It was a bad fall, and Joe began to cry, but he stopped when he saw something on the grass in front of him.

"A treasure map!" he murmured, and he put the crumpled sheet of paper in his pocket.

Mary ran up. "You don't want to play with that boy," she said firmly. "Come on. Let's go down to the beach."

As they hurried away, they heard laughter from the ship, but Joe didn't care. He still had the treasure map.

They came to the top of the dunes, and there
below them lay a wide, sandy beach. A boat was
coming in, and Mary watched it through her
telescope. Joe ran down to have a closer look.

The boat tied up at the end of a jetty. As Joe
ran towards it, a huge hand reached out at him.
Joe gasped and drew back.
But it was only an old fisherman. "Hello there,"
he said, patting Joe on the shoulder, "have you
come to see what I've caught?"
Joe nodded nervously, then quickly ran back
to Mary.

"What's the matter?" asked Mary, surprised at his
pale face.
"The fisherman," said Joe. "I thought he was
a pirate." As he spoke, his hand closed tightly on
the piece of paper in his pocket.
"Don't be silly," said Mary. "There are no pirates
any more. But there's a wreck over there. Shall
we have a look at it?"
They ran down to the water's edge.

Joe stumbled and stubbed his toe on a wooden box.
It was almost hidden beneath a tangle of brown
seaweed. A treasure chest! he thought.

Mary pulled back the lid, but inside there was only
an old fishing net, a newspaper and some shells.
"Not Blackbeard's Treasure," said Joe with a sigh.
"What do you mean?" asked his sister.

Joe spread out his map on the lid of the box.
It showed an island, drawn in red, and across the
top was some curly writing. "Blackbeard's
Treasure," read Mary out loud. "Maybe we can
find it," she said, picking up a shell and turning
it over, thoughtfully, as she spoke.
A tiny starfish fell out of the shell and clattered
onto the box.
"Keep it," said Mary. "It may bring us luck."
Joe wrapped the starfish carefully in the treasure
map and put it in his pocket.

That night, they both slept very soundly, with the treasure map pinned to the wall between their beds, and the starfish nestling on Joe's pillow.

The rest of the holiday passed quickly. As Mary and Joe hunted for the treasure, they met lots of other children who all wanted to join in with the hunt.

Joe and Mary didn't find the treasure, but that didn't matter. It was fun just trying to find it, and playing pirates with all their new friends.

And they never saw the boy with the black bandana again.